Take a Bath!

My Tips for Keeping Clean

Gina Bellisario

illustrated by Holli Conger

M MILLBROOK PRESS • MINNEAPOLIS

For cool Uncle George, and Cristen
and Tet, amazing aunts —G.B.

For O.C. The dirtier you get, the
more fun you have! —H.C.

Millbrook Press
A division of Lerner Publishing Group, Inc.
241 First Avenue North
Minneapolis, MN 55401 U.S.A.

For reading levels and more information, look up this title at
www.lernerbooks.com.

Main body text set in Slappy Inline 18/28.
Typeface provided by T26.

Library of Congress Cataloging-in-Publication Data

Bellisario, Gina.
    Take a bath! : my tips for keeping clean / by Gina Bellisario;
  illustrated by Holli Conger.
       p.   cm. — (Cloverleaf books™ — My healthy habits)
    Includes index.
    ISBN 978–1–4677–1352–8 (lib. bdg. : alk. paper)
    ISBN 978–1–4677–2536–1 (eBook)
    1. Baths—Health aspects—Juvenile literature. 2. Health—
  Juvenile literature. 3. Grooming—Juvenile literature. I. Conger,
  Holli, illustrator. II. Title.
  RA780.B43 2014
  613'.41—dc23   2013018078

Manufactured in the United States of America
1 – BP – 12/31/13

TABLE OF CONTENTS

Chapter One
Mud Monsters

My name is Caleb. This is my dog, Wyatt. We're playing our favorite outside game. Mud Monsters!

Uh-oh! Mom says it's time to get ready for dinner.

I'm too messy to eat.
This mud monster needs a bath first!

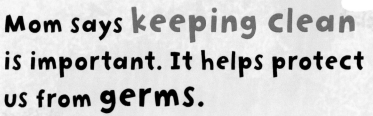

Mom says **keeping clean** is important. It helps protect us from **germs.**

Germs live everywhere. They hang out on doorknobs and grocery carts and even on me and Wyatt.

We can't see germs. But if we could, we'd sure be surprised!

Germs are a big part of our world. But we need a microscope to see them. They are very tiny. Millions of germs can fit on one fingernail.

Mom says if germs get inside our bodies, they can make us **sick**. Some germs cause us to cough and sneeze. Others hurt our stomachs. We can also get a fever.

That means being stuck inside.
And no playing Mud Monsters.

Viruses and bacteria are common kinds of germs. Both can cause many illnesses. But most bacteria are good for you. They help your body get vitamins from food. And they fight bad bacteria that get inside you.

9

Chapter Two

Bubble Trouble

I don't have to be a monster to scare off germs. Mom says there's one thing that makes them run. **Bubble Trouble!**

Dog Shampoo

Germs hide on our bodies. They sneak into warm, dark places. So I wash behind my ears and between my toes.

Wash your paws, Wyatt!

Want to give germs bubble trouble? Try to take a bath or a shower most days. Shampoo your hair at least three times a week. And ask a grown-up to trim your nails. Short nails are easier to keep clean.

Mom helps me dry off with a clean towel. Then I get dressed. I put on clean underwear and socks, clean pants, and a clean shirt.

My dirty clothes go in the washing machine. They need a bath too. Boy, are they **stinky!**

Having clean hands is another part of staying healthy. Be sure to wash up after you get them dirty or use the toilet. First, wet your hands with warm water. Then scrub them well with soap. Scrub for as long as it takes to sing the ABCs. When you're done, rinse off your clean hands.

Chapter Three

No Germ Zone

Mud monsters eat mud pies. But I'm a clean monster now. Mom says we're having macaroni and cheese, fruit salad, and carrots.

Before we have dinner, Mom and I wash our hands. We also wash the fruit and vegetables. That way, germs stay off our food.

Don't let germs share your food. Before eating, soap up at the sink. And keep fingers out of your nose, mouth, eyes, and ears. Use a tissue to catch coughs and sneezes. Or use the inside of your elbow. Tell germs, "Hands OFF!"

We need a clean place to eat. So Mom and I make a **No Germ Zone.**

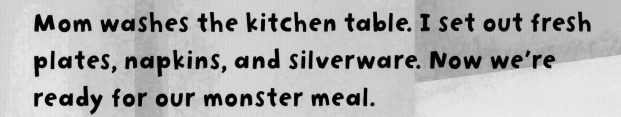

Mom washes the kitchen table. I set out fresh plates, napkins, and silverware. Now we're ready for our monster meal.

YUM!

Do you save lunch box leftovers? Throw them away at school. Bacteria grow in a warm lunch box. By the time you get home, the food is unsafe to eat. And your lunch box is unclean.

Wyatt and I have fun after dinner. Then it's time for bed. That means lights out for mouth **germs.**

Mouth germs snack on food that gets stuck between our teeth. When germs eat, they make a smelly gas. The gas gives us bad breath. That's another reason to brush and floss!

Mom says lots of germs are inside our mouths. They can harm our teeth. I brush my teeth and tongue after breakfast and before bed. And **I floss every night.**

floss

Wyatt's dreaming about going back outside
tomorrow. Me too. But I'll be smart about
germs. This monster knows how to keep clean.

I can play the
healthy way!

Pass the Germs, Please!

Germs like to get around. But they can't travel by themselves. One way they get from place to place is by hitching a ride on our hands. Then they stick to anything we touch. Want to learn how germs get around? Grab some friends or family members. Tell them to pass the germs, please!

What you need:
flour
a bowl
a small object, such as a cup or a potato
any number of people

1) Pour some flour into a bowl. Think of the flour as germs.

2) Place everyone in a circle. Have the youngest person pretend to sneeze into his or her hands. Then ask that person to dip his or her hands into the "germs."

3) Have the person pick up a clean cup or other small object and pass it to his or her right.

4) Keep passing the object from person to person. Make sure everyone takes a turn holding it. After the object is passed to the last person, put it in the bowl.

5) Hold up your hands. Do you see flour on them? This is how germs spread. Wash your hands to stay healthy. Pass the soap, please!

GLOSSARY

bacteria: a kind of germ. Many bacteria are helpful, but some cause illnesses.

floss: to clean between teeth by using dental floss

germs: tiny living things that often cause sicknesses

microscope: a powerful tool that is used to look at very small things

viruses: germs that make people sick

TO LEARN MORE

BOOKS

Heos, Bridget. ***Let's Meet a Doctor.*** Minneapolis: Millbrook Press, 2013.
If you get sick, you may need to see a doctor. Find out what kinds of things doctors do in this book.

Royston, Angela. ***Why Do I Wash My Hands?*** Irvine, CA: QEB Publishing, 2009.
This book has photos of kids cleaning their hands, hair, and more. It has activities that teach you about germs too.

WEBSITES

BAM! Body and Mind
http://www.bam.gov/index.html
Go on a germ-fighting adventure with the Immune Platoon. Learn how your body protects itself from germs that can make you sick.

NSF Scrub Club
http://www.scrubclub.org/site/meet.aspx
Join the Scrub Club, and send germs down the drain! You can play games, print stickers and posters, and sing a hand-washing song.

Sesame Street
http://www.sesamestreet.org/parents/topicsandactivities/topics/hygiene
Watch fun videos about taking a bath and brushing your teeth. You can even learn how to be a hand-washing master!

LERNER SOURCE™
Expand learning beyond the printed book. Download free, complementary educational resources for this book from our website, www.lernerresource.com.

INDEX